# GIDDY-UP BUCKAROOS!

Shanda Trent

Tom Knight

LITTLE TIGER PRESS

London

Giddy-up, **Buckaroos!**
Here comes the sun.

Let's sneak past the sheriff
and round up some fun.

Grab something tasty, uno, dos, tres.

No time to clean up.
Gotta scram from this place.

Dash past
the **lobo**

that lives
in his den.

¡Ándale!
Hurry!
We fooled him again!

A stagecoach! Surround it.
Let's holler and hoot.

Now head for the hills
with this sack
full of loot.

Race 'round these barrels
in cloverleaf loops.

Try not to tip them.
¡Qué lástima!
Oops.

The sheriff! She'll catch us.

Whew.
That was close.

¡Qué bueno!
We lost her.

Giddy-up!
¡Adiós!

Out in the desert.
No agua in sight.
Is there nothing
to quench us?

Here's something
that might!

Plip-plop goes the rain.

Squish-squoosh goes the mud.

The río is rising.
Oh no! A flash flood!

Rescue that lizard.
We flooded his nest.

Buckaroo heroes,
the best in the West!

**Shucks!**
It's the sheriff.
No, don't wash
my shirt!

Cowboys take days to
collect all this dirt.

Our bellies are grumbling
for something to eat.

Follow your nose
to a buckaroo treat.

Roast armadillo.

Yum!
Rattlesnake stew.

BREEZY
BEANS

Here, give our amigo
a bite of it too.

Listen! What's that?
The sheriff is near!

She'll sneak up
and brand us.

¡Venga!
Hide here.

Uh-oh! We're captured.
We can't get away.

Is this **adiós** to our buckaroo day?

Off to the bunkhouse,
we make our retreat.

Hats off our heads,
and boots off our feet.

The night sky is **glowing**
with twinkly stars.

We sing with coyotes
and strum our guitars.

We're wrapped in our bedrolls
and snuggled in tight.
Buckaroo bedtime.

Buenas noches,
goodnight.

# Glossary

**Adiós** *(ah-dee-**oss**)* – Goodbye

**Agua** *(**ah**-gwah)* – Water

**Amigo** *(ah-**mee**-go)* – Friend

**¡Ándale!** *(**an**-da-ley)* – Hurry!

**Buenas noches**
*(**bweh**-nahs **noh**-chehs)* – Goodnight

**¡Caramba!** *(kah-**rahm**-bah)* – Yikes!